WHERE'S MARY'S HAT?

BARROUX

VIKING

Mary's favorite hat was missing.
"How strange," said Mary.
"I'm sure I left it right here."

Mary set out to find her hat.
Before long she saw a stork.
"Hello," said Mary. "I'm afraid I lost my hat.
Have you seen it?"

"No," said the stork.
"But if you hurry, you might ask the goldfish
before he leaves on vacation."

Mary hurried to find the goldfish.

"Excuse me," she said.

"Did you happen to see a lost hat?"

"No," said the goldfish.

"But you could ask the elephant."

Mary walked until she found the elephant.
"Pardon me," said Mary. "I'm afraid I lost my hat.
Have you seen it?"

"No," said the elephant.
"But keep an eye out for the beaver.
He might know something."

Mary looked around.

"Hello up there," she called.

"Did you happen to see a lost hat?"

"No," yelled the beaver.

"But I see a chicken over the next hill. Ask him!"

Soon Mary met up with the chicken.

"Pardon me," she said. "I'm afraid I lost my hat.
Have you seen it?"

"No," said the chicken.
"But you could check with the pig."

"Sorry to interrupt," said Mary.
"Did you happen to see a lost hat?"

"No," said the pig.
"But have you asked the kangaroo?"

The kangaroo was practicing his bunt.
"Excuse me," Mary said.
"I'm afraid I lost my hat. Have you seen it?"

"No," said the kangaroo.
"But maybe the monkeys can help you."

"Good day," said Mary.
"Did you happen to see a lost hat?"

"Sorry," said the monkeys.
"But the rabbit might have. Ask him."

Mary found the rabbit making a pit stop.
"Hello," she said. "I'm afraid I lost my hat.
Have you seen it?"

"No," said the rabbit.
"But have you asked the toucan yet?"

Mary walked along until she saw the toucan.

"Excuse me," she said. "Have you seen a lost hat?"

"Afraid not," said the toucan.

"But maybe the bees know where it is."

The bees were warming up when Mary found them.
"Hello," she said. "I've lost my hat.
Have you seen it?"

"No," said the bees.
"But the penguins might be able to help you."

Dance lessons were in full swing
when Mary saw the penguins.
"Pardon me," she called. "Has anyone seen a lost hat?"

"No," said the penguins.
"But check with the bear.
He might know something."

"Hello," said Mary when she saw the bear.
"I've looked everywhere for my lost hat.
Have *you* seen it?"

"No," said the bear. "I'm afraid not . . ."

“. . . but what do you think of my new kite?”

To Marguerite, Annabelle,
Milan, and Frédérique

VIKING • Published by the Penguin Group • Penguin Putnam Books for Young Readers, 345 Hudson Street,
New York, New York 10014, U.S.A. • Penguin Books Ltd, Registered Offices: Harmondsworth, Middlesex, England
First published in 2003 by Viking, a division of Penguin Putnam Books for Young Readers.
1 3 5 7 9 10 8 6 4 2

LIBRARY OF CONGRESS CATALOGING-IN-PUBLICATION DATA • Barroux, Stephane. Where's Mary's Hat? / Barroux.
p. cm. SUMMARY: When Mary cannot find her favorite hat, she asks one animal after another, but no one has seen it.
ISBN 0-670-03601-3 [1. Animals—Fiction. 2. Lost and found possessions—Fiction. 3. Hats—Fiction.] I. Title.
PZ7.B275675 Wh 2003 [E]—dc21 2002152341
Manufactured in China • Set in Mrs Eaves, Providence • Book design by Teresa Kietlinski